Dexter's Journey

Other titles in the bunch:

Big Dog and Little Dog Go Sailing
Big Dog and Little Dog Visit the Moon
Colin and the Curly Claw
Dexter's Journey
Follow the Swallow
"Here I Am!" said Smedley

Horrible Haircut
Magic Lemonade
The Magnificent Mummies
Midnight in Memphis
Peg
Shoot!

Crabtree Publishing Company
www.crabtreebooks.com

PMB 16A, 350 Fifth Avenue
Suite 3308
New York, NY 10118

612 Welland Avenue
St. Catharines, Ontario
Canada, L2M 5V6

d'Lacey, Chris.
  Dexter's Journey / Chris d'Lacey ; illustrated by David Roberts.
  p. cm. -- (Blue Bananas)
  Summary: When a crate full of yellow plastic ducks is washed
overboard on its journey to America, the ducks are rescued a few at
a time until only Dexter remains, waiting to be found.
  ISBN 0-7787-0846-2 -- ISBN 0-7787-0892-6 (pbk.)
  [1. Ducks--Fiction. 2. Toys--Fiction.] I. Roberts, David, 1970- .
ill. II. Title. III. Series.
PZ7.D6475 De 2002
[E]--dc21
                                        2001032444
                                        LC

Published by Crabtree Publishing in 2002
First published in 2000 by Mammoth
an imprint of Egmont Children's Books Limited
Text copyright © Chris d'Lacey 2000
Illustrations © David Roberts 2000
The Author and Illustrator have asserted their moral rights.
Paperback ISBN 0-7787-0892-6
Reinforced Hardcover Binding ISBN 0-7787-0846-2

2 3 4 5 6 7 8 9 0 Printed in Italy 0 9 8 7 6 5 4 3

Dexter's Journey

Chris d'Lacey

Illustrated by David Roberts

Blue Bananas

For Alice Georgina
because she's quackers!
C.d'L.

For Lauren and Simon
D.R.

Once upon a bath time, there was a yellow plastic duck called Dexter . . .

. . . who was about to go on a long, long journey.

It started on a ship that was sailing to America. Dexter and a lot of other little ducks were packed tightly into a large wooden crate. There was hardly room for a duck to quack.

Suddenly a storm began to blow.

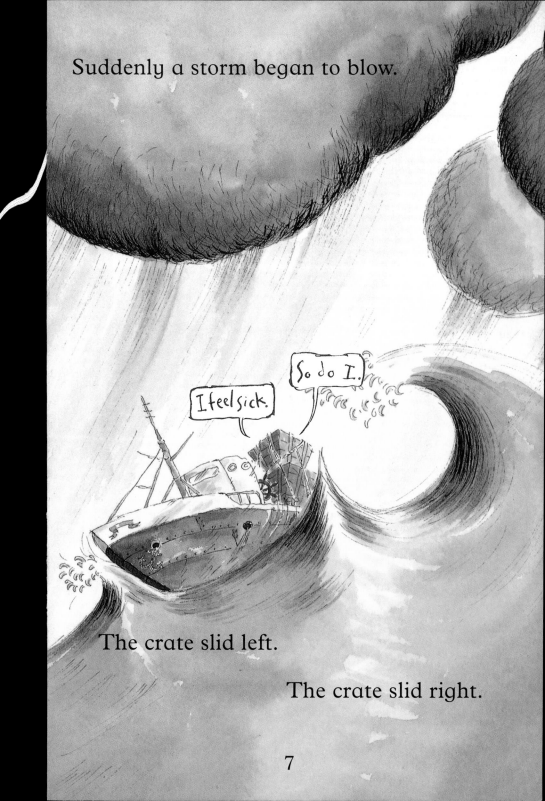

The crate slid left.

The crate slid right.

7

Then . . . CRASH! It slid overboard! And all the little ducks went bobbing out to sea!

One morning, some hungry seagulls appeared. They were circling in the gray sky, searching for food.

They saw the ducks and came swooping down.

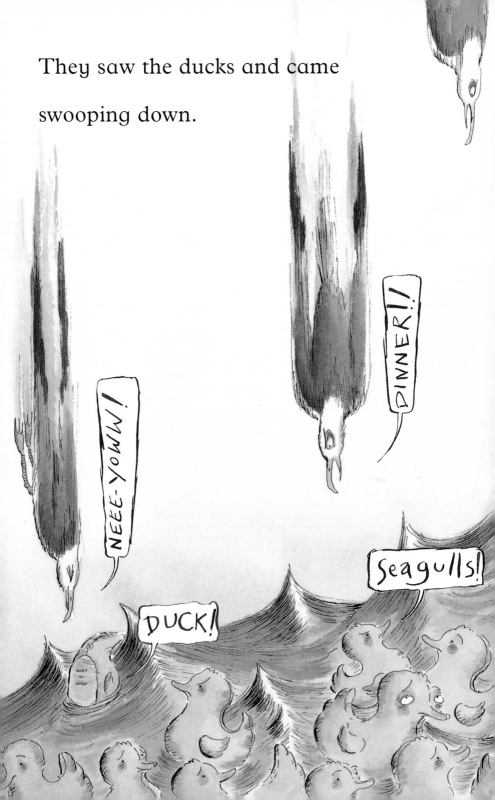

The ducks bobbed bravely but couldn't get away. Dozens were snatched from the open waves and carried away to the seagulls' nests!

So the seagulls went off looking
for fish. The ducks were left all
alone on the cliffs.

It was cold and windy. The sea was crashing on the rocks below. The ducks were frightened, and a little bit dizzy.

Luckily, some rock climbers were out

that day.

They put the ducks safely into their

knapsacks.

Is it a
Computer?

Is it a
bike?

Later, they gave them as
presents to their children.

17

But Dexter was still in the water, bobbing.

That afternoon a fishing boat came
chugging by. It was trailing a great big
net behind it. Hundreds of fish were
wriggling in the net. Soon something
else got in there too . . . .

When the fishermen got home they didn't

know what to do with their catch.

But Old Joe Salty had a good idea.

He took the ducks to a traveling carnival,
so the children could play hook-a-duck
and win them. This made the ducks
very happy.

But Dexter was still on the ocean, bobbing.

Where are we?

Soon, night fell. The moon cast a misty trail across the ocean. It was freezing cold, and getting foggy too. The ducks huddled together and fell fast asleep.

But when morning came there was ice
all around them! The sea had frozen and
the ducks were stuck! Some of them were
even hidden in a snowdrift!

Fortunately, a Norwegian explorer was passing by.

He chipped out all the ducks he could find and piled them up in a heap on his sled. Dexter quacked and quacked but the explorer didn't hear him.

The explorer took the ducks home to
Norway. He showed school children
pictures of where he'd found them . . .

... then gave them one each.

But Dexter was still stuck in the snow.

Soon the Arctic sun came out. The
snowdrift melted and the ice began
to crack. The ducks played a game
of tag between the ice floes.

Then a huge polar bear came wandering by.
He wanted to play his own game of tag!

There was nowhere the ducks could

escape to – except . . .

. . . under the ice! The ducks held their breath and tumbled along. They tumbled towards a tiny, bright hole . . .

Sploop! It was Uluk the hunter's fishing

hole! Uluk was so surprised at his catch,

he nearly fell into the hole!

One by one, Uluk picked the ducks out.
Then he put them into his parka and
took them to a trading post. He swapped
them for a pair of boots!

The merchant put the ducks on the shelves of her store. She sold them to people who came visiting on their vacation.

But Dexter wasn't up for sale. He wasn't
in the trading post . . .

He wasn't in Uluk's fishing hole . .

Dexter was ALL ALONE on the ocean!

He drifted along for days and days.

He saw a few bits of wood

. . . some twinkling stars

. . . a message in a bottle

. . . and two confused shrimp.

Then one morning something came up.

It was a submarine's periscope.

Dexter swam up close to the periscope.

And this is what the crew of the

submarine saw . . .

With a whoosh the submarine rose to the surface. Captain Toffee walked along the hull. "That's not a giant duck!" he laughed. "It's one of those plastic ones that were lost in the storm."

44

And he picked Dexter up and popped him

in his hat . . .

. . . then took him home to his grandson, George.

That was the end of Dexter's journey.

Now he sits in George's bathroom,

thinking about his adventures and

waiting for George to have his bath.